Note to Parents

Look Around!, the Pre-Reader level of the *Now I'm Reading!*™ series, has five stories that are just right for children who want to read but aren't quite ready to sound out words using phonics. All the stories focus on different but familiar early-learning concepts that are based on the common experiences and interests of young children.

Each story is written with text that follows a sequence of words which form a pattern. That pattern is then repeated throughout the story with some simple and predictable variations. The colorful illustrations provide visual clues to the text, allowing your child to "read" with increased confidence.

If your child has not yet mastered the recognition of letters and their sounds, you can help introduce him or her to the alphabet through fun-filled activities. For more information on those activities, refer to the Learning the Alphabet section at the end of this book.

NOW I'M READING!™

LOOK AROUND!

PRE-READER ■ VOLUME 2

Written by Nora Gaydos
Illustrated by BB Sams

Hardcover Bind-up Edition
copyright © 2003, 2006 by innovativeKids®
All rights reserved
Published by innovativeKids®
A division of innovative USA®, Inc.
18 Ann Street
Norwalk, CT 06854
Printed in China

Conceived, developed and designed
by the creative team at innovativeKids®
www.innovativekids.com

For permission to use any
part of this publication, contact
innovativeKids®
Phone: 203-838-6400
Fax: 203-855-5582
E-mail: info@innovativekids.com

Table of Contents

ON THE JOB

ills in this story: Recognizing occupations; Sight words: *I, can, be, a*

I can be a teacher.

I can be a doctor.

I can be a chef.

I can be a builder.

I can be a judge.

I can be an artist.

I can be an actor.

I can be a pilot.

I can be a firefighter.

I can be anything!

BIRTHDAY SHAPES

ls in this story: Recognizing shapes; Sight words: *A, an, looks, like*

A cake looks like a circle.

A hat looks like a triangle.

A balloon looks like an oval.

A flower looks like a star.

A card looks like a rectangle.

A present looks like a square.

A kite looks like a diamond.

A kiss looks like a heart.

A smile looks like a crescent.

A birthday party looks like fun!

■ STORY 3 ■

MY BUSY BODY

s in this story: Recognizing parts of the body; Sight words: *my, is, are, for*

My feet are for kicking.

My legs are for walking.

My hands are for touching.

My arms are for carrying.

My mouth is for eating.

My ears are for hearing.

My nose is for smelling.

My eyes are for seeing.

My head is for thinking.

My body is for hugging!

■ STORY 4 ■

MY FAMILY

ls in this story: Recognizing titles of family members; Sight words: *I, like, to, with, my*

I like to read books with my mom.

I like to rake leaves with my dad.

I like to draw pictures with my sister

like to play games with my brother.

I like to take walks with my grandmo

I like to plant seeds with my grandpa.

I like to make music with my aunt

I like to find shells with my uncle.

I like to catch bugs with my cousin

I love to be with my family!

DRESS UP

s in this story: Recognizing items of clothing; Sight words: *I, my, we, put, on, our*

I put on my pants.

I put on my shirt.

I put on my tie.

I put on my vest.

I put on my skirt.

I put on my sweater.

I put on my socks.

I put on my shoes.

We put on our hats.

We put on a show!

■ ■ ■ ■ ■ How to Use This Book ■ ■ ■ ■

Prepare by reading the stories ahead of time.
Familiarize yourself with the sight words and the concept-related words in each story. By doing this, you can better guide your child to recognize those words in the text.

Discuss each early learning concept. Before reading, look at a story's title page with your child. Talk about the concept and how it relates to your child's own world. Ask your child what he or she knows about the topic. Encourage him or her to make predictions about what the story will be about.

Read each story aloud to your child. Invite your child to look at the pictures as you read the words in the story. To promote a connection between the spoken word and the printed word, point to the words as you read. Point out the repetitive word pattern that appears in each story.

Read each story with your child. Have your child join in and read along with you. Your child will naturally pick up on the patterned, repetitive text in each story.

■ ■ ■ ■ ■ ■ ■ ■ ■ ■ ■ ■ ■ ■ ■ ■ ■ ■ ■

Have your child "read" to you. Encourage your child to use the picture clues and to point to the words as he or she "reads."

Sound out the beginning letters of words. After your child is familiar with the patterned text, focus on the sounds and letters in different words. This will help create a natural bridge to the next step in reading—using phonics.

■ ■ ■ ■ ■ Glossary of Terms ■ ■ ■ ■ ■ ■

Emergent Literacy: An early stage in the development of "conventional literacy" in which children explore and develop the various skills involved in reading and writing.

Consonant Letters: Letters that represent the consonant sounds and, except for *Y*, are not vowels—*B, C, D, F, G, H, J, K, L, M, N, P, Q, R, S, T, V, W, X, Y, Z*.

Decoding: Breaking a word into parts, giving each letter or letter combination its corresponding sound, and then pronouncing the word (sometimes called "sounding out").

Sight Words: Frequently used words, recognized automatically on sight, which do not require decoding (such as *a, the, is,* and so on).

Visual Clues: Distinctive pictures that readers can use to help them identify an unknown word.

Patterned, Repetitive Text: Text that follows a specific sequence or pattern and is repeated throughout the book (such as—*I like red.; I like blue.; I like pink.*).

■ ■ ■ ■ ■ ■ Learning the Alphabet ■ ■ ■ ■

Children learn best when the learning is meaningful and engaging. Help your child discover the letters and sounds that are all around, so he or she can attach meaning and importance to the task of learning the alphabet.

- **Immerse your child in alphabet-rich surroundings:**
  1. Sing alphabet songs.
  2. Read alphabet books and poems.
  3. Display an alphabet strip somewhere in the house.
  4. Practice writing letters using finger paint.

- **Use environmental print with your child:**
  Environmental print is the print we see all around us on commercial signs, billboards, and labels. It's the first print a child recognizes. Encourage your child to identify letters on signs at different places.

- **Make an A-B-C scrapbook:** Get a blank scrapbook and title each page with an alphabet letter. Using your favorite advertisements, food labels, logos, and so on, cut out and glue an example on each page of the alphabet book to promote an association between the letters and the sounds.

■ ■ ■ ■ ■ ■ ■ ■ ■ ■ ■ ■ ■ ■ ■ ■ ■ ■ ■ ■

■ ■ **The Now I'm Reading!™ Series** ■ ■ ■

The *Now I'm Reading!™* series integrates the best of phonics and literature-based reading. Phonics emphasizes letter-sound relationships, while a literature-based approach brings the enjoyment and excitement of a real story. The series has six reading levels:

Pre-Reader: Children "read" simple, patterned, and repetitive text and use picture clues to help them along.

Level 1: Children learn short vowel sounds, simple consonant sounds, and common sight words.

Level 2: Children learn long and short vowel sounds, more consonants and consonant blends, plus more sight word reinforcement.

Level 3: Children learn new vowel sounds with more consonant blends, double consonants, and longer words and sentences.

Level 4: Children learn advanced word skills, including silent letters, multi-syllable words, compound words, and contractions.

Independent: Children are introduced to high-interest topics as they tackle challenging vocabulary words and information by using previous phonics skills.

■ ■ ■ ■ ■ ■ ■ ■ ■ ■ ■ ■ ■ ■ ■ ■ ■ ■

About the Author

Nora Gaydos is an elementary school teacher with more than ten years of classroom experience teaching kindergarten, first grade, and third grade. She has a broad understanding of how beginning readers develop from the earliest stage of pre-reading to becoming independent, self-motivated readers. Nora has a degree in elementary education from Miami University in Ohio and lives in Connecticut with her husband and two sons. Nora is also the author of *Now I Know My ABCs* and *Now I Know My 1, 2, 3's,* as well as other early-learning concept books published by innovativeKids®.